About the Book

THE SUN GOD riding his fiery chariot through the sky, the moon goddess pausing in the night to smile at the forever-sleeping Endymion, Odin's sacrifice of his eye at the well, Thor struggling to regain his magic hammer—these are among the seven myths deftly recreated in William R. Keyser's *Days of the Week*. Each myth is told with a simplified plot and a single unifying theme to show how our English days of the week got their names. Taken from ancient Greek, Nordic, and Roman lore, these adventure stories introduce younger readers to the riches of mythology in a meaningful way. Howard Simon's vivid drawings capture the power and splendor of these intriguing creatures and their bold exploits.

The Days of the Week

by

WILLIAM R. KEYSER

illustrated by

HOWARD SIMON

HARVEY HOUSE, *Publishers*

New York, New York

For my grandson, Michael John

Library of Congress Catalog Card Number 75-27482
Manufactured in the United States of America
ISBN 0-8178-5442-8

Harvey House, Publishers
20 Waterside Plaza
New York, New York 10010

Published in Canada by Fitzhenry and Whiteside, Ltd., Toronto

THE DAYS OF THE WEEK

Darkness blankets the earth. The world sleeps. Unseen, unheard, unfelt, a new day begins. The old day has slipped magically into yesterday. Today begins and tomorrow stands ahead.

At the beginning of the new day stars twinkle in the sky. Planets blaze brightly as they wander their paths among the stars. Moonlight softens the darkness. One by one the stars disappear and the planets fade. The sky turns slowly from black to grey to blue.

Suddenly the sun breaks from the horizon to the east. Clear light bathes the earth. The world awakens as the sun starts its journey from east to west across the sky.

In the evening that journey is over and the sun slips below the western horizon. Dusk hazes the earth. Darkness falls. The world sleeps.

Unseen, unheard, unfelt, the day ends.

In ancient times people watched the daily passage from
dark to light and named their days in honor of the gods
they worshipped. These names were not the same for
each civilization, but most ancient peoples worshipped
the sun, the moon, the stars and planets. They also worshipped individual gods. They believed these gods were
like humans, but wiser, stronger, more courageous and
beautiful than any human could be.

We have seven days in our calendar whose names come
from ancient Roman and Nordic gods. In English they
are:

> Sunday, the sun god's day
> Monday, the day of the moon goddess
> Tuesday, the day of the brave god, Tyr
> Wednesday, the day of Odin, father of the gods
> Thursday, Thor's day, god of thunder
> Friday, the day of the wise and beautiful
>   goddess, Frigga
> Saturday, the day of Saturn, the harvest god.

These early people created stories about their gods. Parents and grandparents told the stories to their children and grandchildren. In turn, they passed them along to new generations.

We call these stories myths. The people who created them were trying to explain the workings of the world as they saw it. The myths in this book retell some of the adventures of the gods for whom our days are named.

The Sun God

SUNDAY

from the Greek myth

Each night a wonderful golden ship sailed around the rim of the world from west to east.

The ancient people believed that the earth was a broad, flat plateau bordered by mountains which separated it from the great sea. From the highest mountains, the gods looked down upon the world, seeing everything.

They alone could observe the nightly passage of the sun god, who sailed in his ship so he could be in the east for his ride through the sky at dawn.

The god of fire had made the golden chariot that was used for this blazing daytime journey. He had also created the wonderful ship. Each day that ship carried the sun god's wife, children, and helpers to the west to meet the god after his heavenly ride. Each night it bore him back to the east upon the peaceful waters of the great sea.

The sun god slept through the night and awoke as the ship arrived at a white sandy beach. Looking up at the mountains, he could see his sister, the goddess of dawn, climbing to the peaks. As she touched the mountain tops, they glowed with a rosy light.

Now it was time for the sun god to prepare for his ride. His helpers harnessed the nine eager horses to the chariot. These horses were dazzling white and breathed flame from their nostrils. The god himself was shining gold like his chariot. Over his gleaming hair he wore a golden helmet. Blinding light shot from his eyes. His clothing was made from a shimmering gauze material, and brilliant rays streamed from his body.

The sun god leaped into his chariot, took the reins, and guided his horses in their swift dash to the sky. As horses, rider, and chariot cleared the mountaintops, their radiance flooded the world with light.

Up, up, up the straining horses pulled the chariot. At noon they reached the highest point in the heavens. Then

they began their descent to the mountains of the west. Evening fell as the chariot sank to a beach below the mountain peaks.

The sun god reined his tired horses to a stop. His waiting helpers unharnessed the great steeds and sent them to pasture until it was time to sail.

When all was ready, the sun god climbed aboard his golden ship and was reunited with his family. The vessel edged out into the currents of the great sea, which caught it and carried it safely to the other side of the world.

Sunday is named for the shining sun god whose flaming journeys through the sky gave daylight to the world.

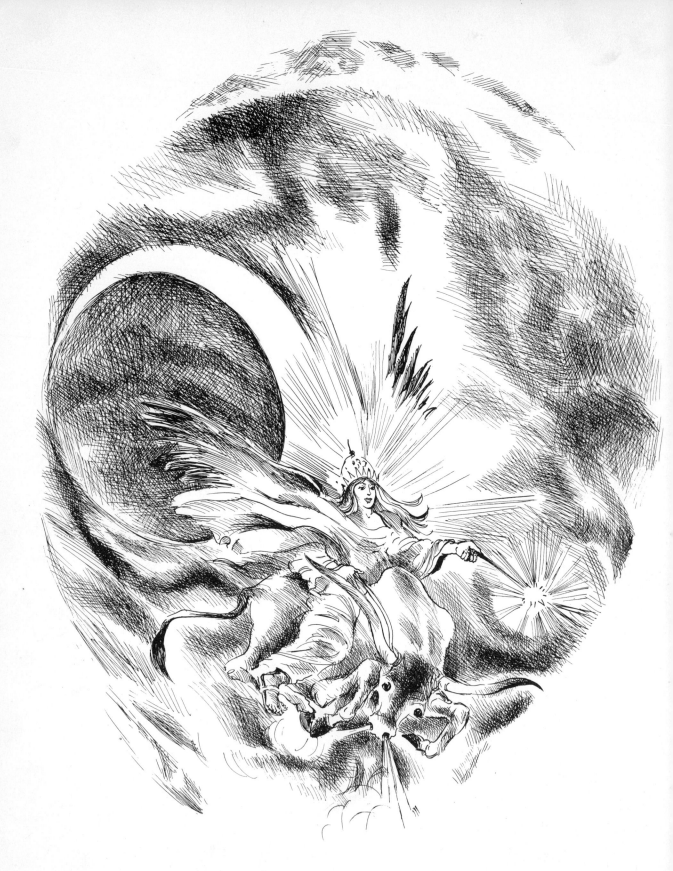

The Moon Goddess

MONDAY

from the Greek myth

The world grew dark after the sun god disappeared from the sky. It was then that the goddess of the moon appeared in the heavens. Her soft, silvery light enchanted the people of the earth. They could sleep and dream peacefully beneath her quiet glow.

The moon goddess was a sister of the sun god. Each night she prepared herself for her journey to the sky after her brother had retired below the mountains to the west.

First she bathed in the cool, fragrant waters of the great sea. Then she dressed in shimmering robes of spun silver, splashed with gleaming jewels. On her fair head she placed a radiant crown. The moon goddess was very beautiful. Her magnificent wings threw a white light all around her.

When she was ready, she called softly to her waiting steed, a pure white bull with silver horns. She climbed upon his shoulders for her gentle ride across the night sky.

15

One very special night, the goddess of the moon was riding peacefully through the heavens. Her light swept softly across the lakes and seas, the mountain slopes, and the fields and streams of the earth. A brook wandering the length of a pasture caught one of her rays and winked it back to her.

The glow of the moon goddess touched the side of a mountain. It crossed a high meadow where deer grazed and rabbits chased their shadows. Suddenly a slight movement at the mouth of a nearby cave caught her attention. She paused to look in. And, at that moment, the moon goddess lost her heart to a mortal man! Endymion, the most handsome prince in all the world, lay sleeping before her. He had climbed mountains and hunted the whole day long. Discovering the cave at evening, he had crawled in to rest from his labors.

The moon goddess marveled at Endymion's beauty. Her glow caressed his face. Before gliding on through the night, she stooped and kissed his lips.

She loved the young man so much that she asked the father of the gods to grant immortality to Endymion. She could not bear the thought that he, as a mortal, someday would die. Her wish was granted only on condition that Endymion remain asleep forever.

The prince never grew old. No lines ever wrinkled his brow. No strands of grey streaked his raven-black hair. And each night the goddess of the moon touched Endymion's face with her soft beams as she paused before the cave where he lay sleeping for all time.

Monday is named for the moon goddess whose gentle light caressed the sleeping world as she came each night to look upon her love.

The Brave God, Tyr

TUESDAY

from the Nordic myth

The courageous god Tyr gave up one of his hands to save the dwellers in Asgard. This is his story.

The ancient people in the north believed their gods lived in a beautiful walled city in the mountains of heaven. In this place, called Asgard, they built huge palaces with many chambers where they lived in peace and harmony.

At certain times trouble disturbed their peaceful lives. One of these troubles was Fenrir, a ferocious wolf. The gods had allowed him to enter Asgard as a pup. They did this because Fenrir was said to be the son of Loki. Loki belonged to the race of evil giants, but Odin, the father of the gods, had made him a blood brother.

The gods had been warned that Fenrir would become one of their worst enemies. This warning began to come true as the wolf grew into a fierce, hungry beast.

The gods came to fear him greatly. Only Tyr was willing to go to Fenrir's den to feed him the great chunks of meat the wolf demanded every evening. Tyr owned a magic sword with which he had defended the city against the attacks of evil giants who wished to destroy the gods. He used the tip of this sword to push the raw meat into the snarling animal's jaws.

The day came when Fenrir frightened the gods so much that they decided they must chain him. They dared not kill him, as that would be wrong to do on holy ground.

Instead they forged heavy chains of the strongest iron. Each time, Fenrir broke loose and ran about the city threatening everyone.

In desperation the gods sought the help of certain dwarfs, who were the most clever craftsmen in the world. They made a chain of magic materials—among them the spit of a bird, the roots of a mountain, the beard of a woman, the sound of a stalking cat, and the breath of a fish.

The gods then went to Fenrir and asked him to test the strength of this new chain. Fenrir was as clever as he was strong and suspected that the new chain was magical. He did not wish to appear cowardly, however, so he agreed to test it if one of the gods would put his hand in his mouth. He thought none of them dared risk this, for if the chain held, Fenrir would surely bite the hand off.

Only brave Tyr stepped forward. He placed his hand between the wolf's jaws. The chain was snapped around Fenrir's neck. He struggled—he pulled—he strained—but the chain held. He knew he was a captive and, in revenge, he snapped his jaws shut and bit off Tyr's hand.

The grateful gods covered Tyr's wound with healing salves. Fenrir remained chained until the end of time. Once more the gods walked without fear along the beautiful streets of Asgard.

Tuesday is named for the god Tyr, who courageously sacrificed his hand in order that his city could be a place of peace and safety.

Odin, Father of the Gods

WEDNESDAY
from the Nordic myth

Odin was the great father of all the gods who dwelled in Asgard. He watched over the world of mortals from his tall watchtower. He decided who would win the battles fought on earth. He had several magic helpers. Two ravens named Hugin and Munin flew over the world each morning before breakfast. They returned and sat on Odin's shoulders to report the news of all things happening. Geri and Freki, two wolves, guarded Odin's watchtower. They sat at his feet during the nightly feasts for the fallen heroes in Valhalla, the largest palace in Asgard. Odin's eight-legged horse, Sleipnir, grazed in the pastures of Asgard. No steed could outrun Sleipnir, who carried Odin on many of his journeys.

On one special journey, however, Odin left all of his magic helpers behind. He was troubled over some of the things happening in the world. He disguised himself and travelled to the Well of Wisdom.

25

No one recognized the old man walking toward the gates of Asgard. He wore a soft, hooded cloak and carried the staff of a common traveller. Heimdall, the watchman at Bifrost, stopped Odin and asked him to identify himself. Bifrost was the rainbow bridge between Asgard and the earth, called Midgard.

Only Mimir, the guardian of the sacred well, recognized him. Mimir drank from the Well of Wisdom every day and knew all things. "Odin, father of the gods, why have you come here?" Mimir asked.

"Last morning," Odin said, "my ravens reported evil times ahead for the world of men. I came to drink from your well to gain the wisdom to help them."

"No one, not even you, Odin, drinks from the Well of Wisdom without making a great sacrifice," Mimir warned.

"What must I do?" Odin asked.

"Give me one of your eyes," Mimir said. "Tear it out and hand it to me. Then you may drink."

Odin tore one of his eyes from its socket and handed it to Mimir. Then he drank from the well.

Thereafter Odin saw more clearly into the future. He saw times of joy, but also times of sorrow and destruction. His new wisdom helped him to accept things that must come to all beings. Now he knew better how to help the world of men.

Mimir dropped Odin's eye into the Well of Wisdom where it remained for all time.

Wednesday is named for the father of the gods, who cared so much for the people of earth that he sacrificed one of his eyes to help them.

Thor, God of Thunder

THURSDAY

from the Nordic myth

Thor, son of Odin, was huge and incredibly strong. He had fierce blue eyes and a bright red beard. Thor travelled in a brass chariot drawn by two goats named Tooth-gnasher and Gap-tooth. Thunder rumbled over the world when Thor drove his chariot across the sky.

The other gods relied on Thor to defend Asgard. He was able to do this because of his enormous strength and his three magic helpers.

The greatest of these helpers was a hammer called Miolnir. It always hit its target and returned to his hand after he threw it. The noise it made when it hit caused thunderbolts to crash across the heavens. Thor's hammer had been forged by the same dwarfs who made the magic chain to bind Fenrir.

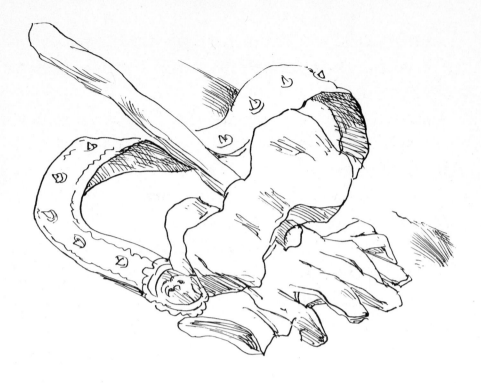

Thor's second helper, his magic gloves, helped him grasp the great hammer.

His magic belt, the third helper, doubled his strength when he buckled it around his waist.

One morning Thor awakened to find his hammer missing. He called for Loki, his mischievous companion, who loved to play tricks on the gods.

During this crisis, however, Loki was very helpful. He suspected that the giant Thrym had stolen the hammer, and flew to the land of the giants on magic wings to talk to the thief.

Thrym admitted stealing the hammer. He said he would return it if the beautiful Freya of Asgard would marry him.

Loki flew back to Asgard with Thrym's words. Freya cried and said she would never marry such an ugly being.

The other gods, who loved her very much, said she did not have to. They decided, however, that the hammer must be returned.

Then Loki suggested a trick—that Thor dress as Freya, cover his head and face with a bridal veil, and go to Thrym disguised as a bride. The mighty Thor, hurler of thunderbolts, could think of nothing worse than dressing as a woman, but he finally agreed.

Thrym danced for joy when he learned that Freya had consented to be his bride. He prepared a huge feast for her and her bridesmaid, who was really Loki, dressed as a woman.

As soon as Thor and Loki entered his castle, Thrym tried to steal a kiss, but Thor drew the veil tightly around his face. Loki told Thrym that Freya was too shy to accept a kiss before she was married.

At dinner Thor, who was sitting with the women, devoured everything in sight—an entire ox, eight salmon, and all the vegetables, salads, and desserts on the table. Thrym was surprised at his bride's enormous appetite. Loki explained that Freya was so excited about the wedding that she had not eaten for a week.

After the banquet, Thrym again tried to kiss his beloved. Loki demanded that the wedding be held first, and that before the wedding Miolnir be given to the bride as Thrym had agreed.

Thrym left the hall and returned shortly with the hammer. He placed it on the knees of his bride-to-be. At that moment, Thor threw off his veil and grasped Miolnir in his mighty fist. He swung it right and left like a sword, destroying all the giants in Thrym's castle.

Thursday is named for Thor, the thunder god who disguised himself as a bride to win back his powerful hammer.

The Goddess Frigga

FRIDAY

from the Nordic myth

Frigga, the most beloved goddess in Asgard, and the wife of the great father, Odin, was always busy. Early each morning she planned the nightly banquets at Valhalla for Odin's fallen heroes. While spinning the many spools of thread needed for her loom, she composed poetry and songs. She trimmed the loose threads from the cloth she wove and cast them aside. Lucky indeed was the earth woman who found one, for she would never again run out of thread.

When Frigga spun the colors for the sunset sky, she used threads of silver and gold, lacing them with jewels. She knew all things that happened. Some gave her joy, some brought sadness. If Frigga was happy, the sunset blazed with glorious colors. If she was sad, the sky was subdued and grey.

Frigga loved the people of earth and shared their joys and sorrows. She helped them when she could. Once she had to play a trick on Odin to help them. Here is how it happened.

Two powerful tribes were fighting a great war. The Vangards were overrunning the Winniles as night fell, but Odin had not determined which tribe would win. He decided to sleep and award the victory to the army he first sighted when he awakened.

During the night, the women and children of the Winniles prayed to Frigga to help them. Frigga heard their prayers and was moved.

She dressed in her magic cape of pale blue falcon feathers and flew down behind the Winniles' battle lines. Then she told the women what they must do.

The next morning Odin awakened and peered out his window. He saw what he thought was a band of soldiers with long black beards. He rubbed his eye and looked again. He was very puzzled, for he thought he knew all the soldiers in the world by sight.

"What tribe is this I see before me?" he muttered. "I should know these warriors, but I don't recognize them!"

Then he chuckled to himself. "It must be too early in the morning for me to see well. I will just guess who they are—they are the Longbeards."

Frigga then signalled the women to reveal themselves. Dressed in the armor of their fallen men, their long hair pulled under their chins to resemble beards, they had fooled Odin.

Odin looked embarrassed, but he quickly came to a fair decision. "So, you're not Longbeards," he said. "You are Winniles. Because I called you Longbeards, that will be your new name. And since you were the first army I saw when I awakened, the victory is yours. Go home. Your soldiers have won the battle."

The women thanked Frigga and Odin and returned to their homeland rejoicing. From that time their people have been called the Longbeards.

Friday is named for the household goddess Frigga, who cleverly saved a homeland for a grateful people.

Saturn, the Harvest God

SATURDAY

from the Roman myth

Can a god who was said to have eaten his own children come to be regarded as a kind, loveable teacher? According to ancient legends, Saturn was such a god.

At one time Saturn lived in the skies where he was the god of time. Even today one of our solar planets bears his name. As the god of time, he ended all things, just as Saturn's day still ends the week.

Saturn had many sons and daughters, but he devoured them as soon as they were born. He was afraid that they might grow up to become his rivals. One of his sons escaped this fate, however, as his mother hid him away. This son was Jupiter, who returned to banish his father from the heavens to earth.

Saturn's land of exile was the sunny, beautiful country around Rome, a land of high mountains, low hills, and

fertile plains. Saturn taught the people how to reap rich harvests from their vineyards and fields. He showed them how to sow crops, how to tend them, and how to harvest them when they were ripe.

The people honored Saturn by holding a festival at the end of the harvest season. It lasted seven days and they called it *Saturnalia*. Everyone celebrated the festival. On the day it began, children left school shouting "Happy Saturnalia" to each other. Merchants closed their shops, soldiers came home on leave, and even the slaves enjoyed seven days of freedom.

Religious ceremonies opened the Saturnalia festival. Farmers prepared their best piglets, townspeople carried their finest weavings to the temples to offer them to Saturn and to pray, "Saturn, stay with us always."

Then the feasting began. And such feasts! They lasted all day, every day. Masters waited on their slaves, bringing them the choicest morsels.

Families and friends exchanged gifts. A small doll with a tiny sickle clutched in its hand was always included among them. The doll represented Saturn harvesting grain.

The people made statues of Saturn and tied them to the temple columns to make sure that Saturn would not leave them.

After the Saturnalia ended, winter settled in. People rested and waited for the coming of spring when, again, they would plant as Saturn had taught them.

Saturday is named for the harvest god who showed the people how to grow and reap rich crops from the earth.

AN AFTERWORD

Many years have passed since our ancestors named the days to honor their gods. Many things have changed since then, including the names of the gods themselves.

Tyr became Tiw
Odin became Woden
Thor became Thur
Frigga became Friga

The language we speak changed. So did the spelling and pronunciation of the word *day*. The table below shows the differences in the names of the days over the last 1,500 years.

Old English 450 to 1150 A.D.	Middle English 1150 to 1475 A.D.	Modern English
Sunnandaeg	Sun(nen)day	Sunday
Mon(an)daeg	Mone(n)day	Monday
Tiwesdaeg	Tewesday	Tuesday
Wodnesdaeg	Wednesdai	Wednesday
Thursdaeg	Thursdaeg	Thursday
Frigadaeg	Frigedaeg	Friday
Sater(nes)daeg	Saterdaeg	Saturday

Still, some things have not changed.

We no longer worship the gods for whom the days were named, but we remember them. Each day the sun breaks from the eastern horizon, reminding us of the sun god driving his winged chariot across the heavens. The moon sails serenely through the dark night sky, caressing faces as it did Endymion's. We, like the gods in Asgard, admire bravery such as Tyr's. Wisdom is as difficult to acquire now as it was in the time of Odin's trip to Mimir's well. Thunder still shakes earth and sky, recalling Thor and his magic hammer. The brilliance of a sunset sky brings joy to us today as it did to Frigga when she was happy. And each week comes full circle with Saturn's day.

Each day slips magically into yesterday. Today begins and tomorrow stands ahead.

About the Author

WILLIAM R. KEYSER has spent his adult life in the worlds of language and literature. Following his graduation from Ohio's Marietta College, he served as a navigator on B-17's in the United States Air Force. After training at the Presidio of Monterey Army Language School in California, where he became fluent in Persian, he served in Iran for three years as an attaché to the U.S. Embassy.

For the past 20 years Mr. Keyser has worked in publishing. This book, his first, was inspired by his studies of ancient civilizations while in the Middle East.

About the Artist

HOWARD SIMON has been an internationally acclaimed artist for many years. He is the illustrator of over 90 books for adults and young readers. His paintings and woodcuts are owned by many museums and private collectors throughout the world, including the New York Metropolitan Museum of Art and the New York Public Library Prints Division.

Mr. Simon lives at the foothills of the Berkshires in upstate New York. He is currently teaching art at Barlow School in Amenia, New York and working on a series of wood blocks on the Creation according to the Book of Genesis.